John S. Winter, Mrs. Molesworth, Frances E. Crompton

A Christmas Fairy - by John Strange Winter

and other stories

John S. Winter, Mrs. Molesworth, Frances E. Crompton

A Christmas Fairy - by John Strange Winter
and other stories

ISBN/EAN: 9783337227845

Printed in Europe, USA, Canada, Australia, Japan

Cover: Foto ©Andreas Hilbeck / pixelio.de

More available books at **www.hansebooks.com**

A CHRISTMAS FAIRY

*" . A tall handsome lady came in
and Shivers flew to her arms."*

CHRISTMAS FAIRY

BY

JOHN STRANGE WINTER

AND OTHER STORIES BY

FRANCES E. CROMPTON

AND

MRS MOLESWORTH

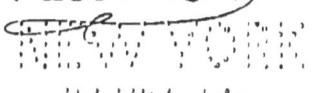
London
Ernest Nister

E. P. Dutton & Co

Printed in Bavaria
878.

A Christmas Fairy

By John Strange Winter.

IT was getting very near to Christmas-time, and all the boys at Miss Ware's school were talking excitedly about going home for the holidays, of the fun they would have, the presents they would receive on Christmas morning, the tips from Grannies, Uncles, and Aunts, of the pantomimes, the parties, the never-ending joys and pleasures which would be theirs.

"I shall go to Madame Tussaud's and to the Drury Lane pantomime," said young Fellowes, "and my mother will give a party, and Aunt Adelaide will give another, and Johnny Sanderson and Mary Gréville, and ever so many others. I shall have a splendid time at home. Oh! Jim, I wish it were all holidays like it is when one's grown up."

"My Uncle Bob is going to give me a pair of skates – clippers," remarked Harry Wadham.

"My father's going to give me a bike," put in George Alderson.

"Will you bring it back to school with you?" asked Harry.

"Oh! yes, I should think so, if Miss Ware doesn't say no."

"I say, Shivers," cried Fellowes, "where are you going to spend your holidays?"

"I'm going to stop here," answered the boy called Shivers, in a very forlorn tone.

"Here—with old Ware?—oh, my! Why can't you go home?"

"I can't go home to India," answered Shivers—his real name, by the bye, was Egerton, Tom Egerton.

"No—who said you could? But haven't you any relations anywhere?"

Shivers shook his head. "Only in India," he said miserably.

"Poor old chap; that's rough luck for you. Oh, I'll tell you what it is, you fellows, if I couldn't go home for the holidays—especially at Christmas—I think I'd just sit down and die."

"Oh! no, you wouldn't," said Shivers; "you'd hate it, and you'd get ever so home-sick and miserable, but you wouldn't die over it. You'd just get through somehow, and hope something would happen before next year, or that some kind fairy or other would——"

"Bosh! there are no fairies nowadays," said Fellowes. "See here, Shivers, I'll write home and ask my mother if she won't invite you to come back with me for the holidays."

"Will you really?"

"Yes, I will: and if she says yes, we shall have such a splendid time, because, you know, we live in London, and go to everything, and have heaps of tips and parties and fun."

"Perhaps she will say no," suggested poor little Shivers.

who had steeled himself to the idea that there would be no Christmas holidays for him, excepting that he would have no lessons for so many weeks.

"My mother isn't at all the kind of woman who says no," Fellowes declared loudly.

In a few days' time, however, a letter arrived from his mother, which he opened eagerly.

"My own darling boy," it said, "I am so very sorry to have to tell you that dear little Aggie is down with scarlet fever, and so you cannot come home for your holidays, nor yet bring your young friend with you, as I would have loved you to do if all had been well here. Your Aunt Adelaide would have had you there, but her two girls have both got scarlatina—and I believe Aggie got hers there, though, of course, poor Aunt Adelaide could not help it. I did think about your going to Cousin Rachel's. She most kindly offered to invite you, but, dear boy, she is an old lady, and so particular, and not used to boys, and she lives so far from anything which is going on that you would be able to go to nothing, so your father and I came to the conclusion that the very best thing that you could do under the circumstances is for you to stay at Miss Ware's and for us to send your Christmas to you as well as we can. It won't be like being at home, darling boy, but you will try and be happy—won't you, and make me feel that you are helping me in this dreadful time. Dear little Aggie is very ill, very ill indeed. We have two nurses. Nora and Connie are shut away in the morning-room and to the back stairs and their own rooms with Miss Ellis, and have not seen us since the dear child was first taken ill. Tell your young friend that I am sending you a hamper from Buszard's, with double of everything, and I am writing to Miss Ware to ask her to take you both to anything that may be

going on in Cross Hampton. And tell him that it makes me
so much happier to think that you won't be alone.—
                              "Your own MOTHER."

"This letter will smell queer, darling; it will be fumigated
before posting."

It must be owned that when Bertie Fellowes received
this letter, which was neither more nor less than a shattering
of all his Christmas hopes and joys, that he fairly broke down,
and hiding his face upon his arms as they rested on his desk,
sobbed aloud. The forlorn boy from India, who sat next to
him, tried every boyish means of consolation that he could
think of. He patted his shoulder, whispered many pitying
words, and, at last, flung his arm across him and hugged him
tightly, as, poor little chap, he himself many times since his
arrival in England, had *wished* someone would do to him.

At last Bertie Fellowes thrust his mother's letter into his
friend's hand. "Read it," he sobbed.

So Shivers made himself master of Mrs. Fellowes' letter
and understood the cause of the boy's outburst of grief. "Old
fellow," he said at last, "don't fret over it. It might be
worse. Why, you might be like me, with your father and
mother thousands of miles away. When Aggie is better, you'll
be able to go home—and it'll help your mother if she thinks
you are *almost* as happy as if you were at home. It must be
worse for her—she has cried ever so over her letter—see, it's
all tear-blots."

The troubles and disappointments of youth are bitter
while they last, but they soon pass, and the sun shines again.
By the time Miss Ware, who was a kind-hearted, sensible,
pleasant woman, came to tell Fellowes how sorry she was for
him and his disappointment, the worst had gone by, and the
boy was resigned to what could not be helped.

"Well, after all, one man's meat is another man's poison," she said, smiling down on the two boys; "poor Tom has been looking forward to spending his holidays all alone with us, and now he will have a friend with him. Try to look on the bright side, Bertie, and to remember how much worse it would have been if there had been no boy to stay with you."

"I can't help being disappointed, Miss Ware," said Bertie, his eyes filling afresh and his lips quivering.

"No, dear boy, you would be anything but a nice boy if you were not. But I want you to try and think of your poor mother, who is full of trouble and anxiety, and to write to her as brightly as you can, and tell her not to worry about you more than she can help."

"Yes," said Bertie; but he turned his head away, and it was evident to the school-mistress that his heart was too full to let him say more.

Still, he was a good boy, Bertie Fellowes, and when he

wrote home to his mother it was quite a bright every-day
kind of letter, telling her how sorry he was about Aggie, and
detailing a few of the ways in which he and Shivers meant
to spend their holidays. His letter ended thus:—

"Shivers got a letter from his mother yesterday with
three pounds in it: if you happen to see Uncle Dick, will
you tell him I want a 'Waterbury' dreadfully?"

The last day of the term came, and one by one, or two
by two, the various boys went away, until at last only Bertie
Fellowes and Shivers were left in the great house. It had
never appeared so large to either of them before. The school-
room seemed to have grown to about the size of a church,
the dining-room, set now with only one table instead of three
was not like the same, while the dormitory, which had never
before had any room to spare, was like a wilderness. To Bertie
Fellowes it was all dreary and wretched—to the boy from
India, who knew no other house in England, no other thought
came than that it was a blessing that he had one companion
left. "It is miserable," groaned poor Bertie as they strolled
into the great echoing school-room after a lonely tea, set at
one corner of the smallest of the three dining-tables; "just
think if we had been on our way home now—how different!"

"Just think if I had been left here by myself," said
Shivers—and he gave a shiver which fully justified his name.

"Yes—but——" began Bertie, then shamefacedly and with
a blush, added, "you know, when one wants to go home ever
so badly, one never thinks that some chaps haven't got a home
to go to."

The evening went by—discipline was relapsed entirely and
the two boys went to bed in the top empty dormitory, and
told stories to each other for a long time before they went
to sleep. That night Bertie Fellowes dreamt of Madame
Tussaud's and the great pantomime at Drury Lane, and poor

Shivers of a long creeper-covered bungalow far away in the shining East, and they both cried a little under the bed-clothes. Yet each put a brave face on their desolate circumstances to the other, and so another day began.

This was the day before Christmas Eve, that delightful day of preparation for the greatest festival in all the year— the day when in most households there are many little mysteries afoot, when parcels come and go, and are smothered

away so as to be ready when Santa Claus comes his rounds; when
some are busy decking the rooms with holly and mistletoe;
when the cook is busiest of all, and savoury smells rise from
the kitchen, telling of good things to be eaten on the morrow.

There were some preparations on foot at Minchin House,
though there was not the same bustle and noise as is to be
found in a large family. And quite early in the morning came
the great hamper of which Mrs. Fellowes had spoken in her
letter to Bertie. Then just as the early dinner had come to
an end, and Miss Ware was telling the two boys that she
would take them round the town to look at the shops, there
was a tremendous peal at the bell of the front door, and
a voice was heard asking for Master Egerton. In a trice
Shivers had sprung to his feet, his face quite white, his hands
trembling, and the next moment the door was thrown open,
and a tall handsome lady came in, to whom he flew with a
sobbing cry of "Aunt Laura! Aunt Laura!"

Aunt Laura explained in less time than it takes me to
write this, that her husband, Colonel Desmond, had had left
to him a large fortune and that they had come as soon as possible to England, having, in fact, only arrived in London the
previous day. "I was so afraid, Tom darling," she said in
ending, "that we should not get here till Christmas Day was
over, and I was so afraid you might be disappointed, that
I would not let Mother tell you we were on our way home.
I have brought a letter from Mother to Miss Ware—and you
must get your things packed up at once and come back with
me by the six o'clock train to town. Then Uncle Jack and
I will take you everywhere, and give you a splendid time,
you dear little chap, here all by yourself."

For a minute or two Shivers' face was radiant; then he
caught sight of Bertie's down-drooped mouth, and turned to
his Aunt.

"Dear Aunt Laura," he said, holding her hand very fast with his own, "I'm awfully sorry, but I can't go."

"Can't go? and why not?"

"Because I can't go and leave Fellowes here all alone," he said stoutly, though he could scarcely keep a suspicious quaver out of his voice. "When I was going to be alone,

Fellowes wrote and asked his mother to let me go home with him, and she couldn't, because his sister has got scarlet fever, and they daren't have either of us; and he's got to stay here - and he's never been away at Christmas before —and—and—I can't go away and leave him by himself, Aunt Laura—and—"

For the space of a moment or so, Mrs. Desmond stared

at the boy as if she could not believe her ears; then she caught hold of him and half smothered him with kisses.

"Bless you, you dear little chap, you shall not leave him: you shall bring him along and we'll all enjoy ourselves together. What's his name?—Bertie Fellowes! Bertie, my man, you are not very old yet, so I'm going to teach you a lesson as well as ever I can—it is that kindness is never wasted in this world. I'll go out now and telegraph to your mother—I don't suppose she will refuse to let you come with us."

A couple of hours later she returned in triumph, waving a telegram to the two excited boys.

"*God bless you, yes, with all our hearts*," it ran; "*you have taken a load off our minds.*"

And so Bertie Fellowes and Shivers found that there was such a thing as a fairy after all.

Part 1

HELENA FRERE and her two younger brothers, Willie and Leigh, were on the whole very good children. They were obedient and affectionate and very truthful. Perhaps it was not very difficult for them to be good, for they had a happy home, wise and kind parents, and a quiet regular life. None of them had ever been at school, for Mrs. Frere liked home teaching best for girls, and the little boys were as yet too young for anything else. Willie was only seven and a half, and Leigh six. Helena was nearly ten.

They lived in the country—quite in the country, and a rather lonely part too. So they had almost no companions of their own age, and the few there were within reach they seldom saw. One family in the neighbourhood, where there were children, always spent seven months abroad; another home was saddened by the only son being a cripple and unable to walk or play; and the boys and girls of a third family were rather too old to be playfellows with our little people.

"It really seems," said Helena sometimes, "it really seems as if I was never to have a proper friend of my own. It's much worse for me than for Willie and Leigh, for they've got each other," which was certainly true.

Still, she was not at all an unhappy little girl, though she was very sorry for herself sometimes, and did not always quite agree with her Mother when she told her that it was better to have no companions than any whom she could not thoroughly like.

"I don't know that, Mamma," Helena would reply. "It would be nice to have other little girls to play with, even if they weren't quite perfection."

You can easily believe therefore that there was great excitement and delight when these children heard, one day, that a new family was coming to live in the very next house to theirs—only about half a mile off, by a short cut across the Park—and that in this family there were children! There were four—Nurse said three, and old Mrs. Betty at the lodge, who was Nurse's aunt, and rather a gossip, said four. But both were sure of one thing—that the newcomers—the children of the family, that is to say—were just about the right ages for "our young lady and gentlemen."

And before long, Helena and her brothers were able to tell Nurse and Mrs. Betty more than they had told them. For Mrs. Frere called at Halling Wood, which was the name of the neighbouring house, and a few days afterwards, Mrs. Kingley returned her call, and fortunately found the children's Mother at home. So all sorts of questions were asked and answered, and when Helena and the boys came in from their walk, Mrs. Frere had a whole budget of news for them.

There were *four* Kingleys, but the eldest was a girl of sixteen, whom the children put aside at once as "no good," and listened impatiently to hear about the others.

"Next to Sybil," said their Mother, "comes Hugh; he is four years younger—only twelve—and then Freda, nearly eleven, and lastly Maggie, a 'tom-boy,' her Mother calls her, of eight."

"I shall like her awfully if she's a tom-boy," said Helena

very decidedly, while Willie and Leigh looked rather puzzled. They had never heard of a tom-boy before, and could not make out if it meant a boy or a girl, till afterwards, when Helena explained it to them, and then Willie said he had thought it must mean a girl, "'cos of Maggie being a girl's name."

"I hope you will like them all," said Mrs. Frere. "By their Mother's account they seem to be very hearty, sensible

children; indeed, she says they are just a little wild, for she
and Mr. Kingley have been a great deal abroad, and the
three younger children were for two years with a lady, who
was rather too old to look after them properly."

"How dreadfully unhappy they must have been," said
Helena, in a tone of pity.

"No," said her Mother, "I don't think they were unhappy. On the contrary, they were rather spoilt and
allowed to run wild. Of course I am telling you this just as
a very little warning, in case Hugh and his sisters ever pro-
pose to do anything you do not think I should like. Do
not give in for fear of vexing them; they will like you all
the better in the end if they see you try to be as good
and obedient out of sight, as when your Father and I are
with you. Do you understand, dears?"

"Yes," said Helena, "of course we won't do anything
naughty, Mamma," though in her heart she thought that
"running wild" sounded rather nice.

"And you, boys?" added their Mother, "do you understand, too?"

"Yes, Mamma," they said, Willie adding, "If you're not
there or Nurse, we'll do whatever Nelly says."

"That's right," said Mrs. Frere. "Nelly, you hear?—
the responsibility is on your shoulders, you see, dear," but
she smiled brightly. For she felt sure that Helena was to
be trusted.

It had been arranged by the two Mammas that the
three Kingley children were to spend the next afternoon at
Halling Park, the Freres' home. They were to come early,
between two and three, and their Mother and Sybil would
drive over to fetch them about five. Some other friends
of Mrs. Frere's were expected too, which would give Mrs.
Kingley an opportunity of meeting her new neighbours.

"Must we have our best things on then, Mamma?" asked Helena, rather dolefully.

Mrs. Frere glanced at her. It was full summer-time—late in June. The little girl looked very nice in a pretty pink-and-white cotton, though it could not have passed muster as perfectly fresh and spotless.

"No," she said, "a clean frock like the one you have on will do quite well—or stay, yes, a white frock would be nicer. And tell Nurse that the boys may wear their white serge suits—it is so nice and dry out-of-doors I don't think they could get dirty if they tried."

And, as I have said already, the little Freres were not at all "wild" children.

To-morrow afternoon came at last, and with it, to the delight of Helena and her brothers, the expected guests. They arrived in a pony-cart, driven by Hugh, who seemed quite in his element as a coachman, and they all three jumped out very cleverly without losing any time about it. Mrs. Frere and *her* three were waiting for them on the lawn, but anyone looking on would have thought that the Kingleys were the "at home" ones of the party, for they shook hands in the heartiest way, and began talking at once, while the little Freres all seemed shy and timid, and almost awkward.

Their Mother felt just a little vexed with them. Then she said to herself that she must remember how very seldom they had had any playfellows, and that it was to be expected they would feel a little strange.

"I daresay you will enjoy playing out of doors far more than in the house, as it is such a lovely day," she said. "Your Mamma and Sybil will be coming before very long, will they not?" she added, turning to Freda.

"About four o'clock," Freda replied; "but I don't want

four o'clock to come too soon; we should like a good long
time for playing first."

Mrs. Frere smiled.

"Well, it is scarcely half-past two yet," she said. "When
four o'clock or half-past four comes, I daresay you will *not*
feel sorry, for you will have had time to get hungry by then."

"All right," said Freda; "come along then, Nelly," for
she had already caught up Helena's short name. "Hugh
and Maggie and I have got heaps of fun in our heads."

She caught hold of Helena's hand as she spoke and
started off, the others following. Mrs. Frere stood looking
after them with a smile, though there was a little anxiety
in her face too.

"I hope they will be careful," she thought; "I can
trust Helena, but these children *are* rather overpowering.
Still, it would scarcely have done to begin checking them the
moment they arrived."

Part 2

HE grounds of Halling Park were very large, the lawns and flower-beds near the house were most carefully kept, and just now in their full summer beauty. The first thought of the little Freres was to show their new friends all over this ornamental part, for the Halling roses were rather famed, and Helena knew the names of the finest and rarest among them.

But Freda Kingley flew past the rosebeds without stopping or letting Helena stop, and, excited by her example, the three boys and Maggie came rushing after them, till the run almost grew into a race, so that when at last the very active young lady condescended to pull up to take breath, Helena was redder and hotter than she had ever been before in her life. Indeed, for a moment or two, she was almost frightened—her heart beat so fast, and there was such a "choky" feeling in her throat. She could not speak, but stood there gasping.

Freda burst out laughing.

"I say," she exclaimed, "you're in very bad condition; isn't she, Hugh?"

Helena stared, which made Freda laugh still more, Hugh joining her.

"I don't understand what you mean," said the little girl at last, when she could speak.

"Oh, it's nothing you need mind," said Hugh good-naturedly. "It only means you're not up to much running—you've not been training yourself for it. Freda was nearly as bad once, before I went to school; she didn't understand, you see. But the first holidays I took her in hand, and she's not bad now—not for a girl. I'll take you in hand if you like."

"Thank you," said Helena; "no, I don't think I want to be taken in hand. I don't care to run so fast. Won't you come back again to see the flowers near the house? And the tennis-court is very nice for puss-in-the-corner or Tom Tiddler's ground."

"We know a game or two worth scores of those old-fashioned things—don't we, Freda?" said Hugh. "But I daresay the tennis-ground's rather jolly, if it's a good big one; we can look it up later on. First of all I want to see the stream. We caught sight of it; it looks jolly enough."

"And there's a bridge across it," said Maggie, speaking for the first time, "a ducky little bridge. It would be fun to stand on it and throw stones down to make the fishes jump."

Willie broke in at this.

"The fish aren't so silly," he said. "The water-hens would scatter away, I daresay, if you threw stones. But Papa doesn't like us to startle them, so it would be no good trying."

"Water-hens!" exclaimed the Kingley children all together. "What are they like? Do let's go and look at them. We've never seen any."

"And most likely we won't see them now," said Helena.

"They're very shy creatures. And we mustn't startle them, as Willie says."

"Oh, bother!" said Freda; "it wouldn't hurt them for once. And who would know? Anyway, let's go to the bridge."

And off she set again, though not quite so fast. Indeed, it would have been impossible to race as she had done across the lawn, for the way to the stream from where they were standing, lay across very high ground, though there was a proper path, or road, leading to the bridge if they had not come by the "cross-country" route.

It was very pretty when they got there, so wild and picturesque—you could have imagined yourself miles and miles away from any house, in some lonely stretch of country. Even the restless Kingley children were struck by it, and stood still in admiration for about a quarter of a minute.

"I say, it's awfully jolly here," said Hugh. "I wish we had a stream and a bridge like this in our grounds."

But almost immediately he began fidgeting about again —leaning over, till Helena felt sure he would tumble in, and twisting himself about to see what there was to be seen below them.

"I know what *would* be fun," said Freda suddenly.

"What?" exclaimed the others.

"Wading," she replied. "If we clamber down the side of the bank—it isn't so very steep—we could get right under the bridge. There's a bit of dry ground at each side of the water, isn't there, Hugh? We could make that our dressing-room, or our bathing-van, whichever you like to call it."

"But," interrupted Helena, "you couldn't undress; we've no bathing-dresses, and——"

"How stupid you are!" interrupted Freda, in her turn. "We'd have to take off our shoes and stockings, of course,

and we can't do that on the sloping bank; under the bridge
is just the place. And we can pretend it's the sea, and that
we're going to bathe properly, and shiver and shudder and
push each other in. Oh! it'll be great fun—come along,
all of you, do."

And somehow she got them all to go—not that she
had any difficulty in persuading her own brother and sister;
they were, as they would themselves have expressed it,
"up to anything"; but the three Freres knew quite well
that it was not the sort of play—especially for Helena—that
their Mother would have approved of. It was very muddy
down under the bridge, and the paddling about in cold
fresh water, when one is already overheated, is not a very
wholesome thing to do. Nor were they dressed for this
sort of play.

But Freda and Hugh had got the upper hand of them.
Helena could not bear to be laughed at, and Willie was terribly
afraid of being thought "soft" by a real schoolboy like Hugh.

It was not so easy to get down by the bank without
accidents, and before they reached the "dressing-room,"
frocks and knickerbockers already told a tale.

"Never mind," said Freda, "it'll brush off when it's dry,
and even if it doesn't quite, you can't be expected never
to get the least bit dirty. Now let's get off our shoes and
stockings as quick as we can," and down she plumped and
began unbuttoning her own boots without further ado.

"I think I'd rather not wade," said Helena.

"Oh, what rubbish!" cried Freda. "In I'll go first and
show you how jolly it is," and in another moment, in she
went, paddling about on the firmer ground in the middle of
the stream, after some very muddy slips or slides to get there.

"It's all right once you get out here," she called back.
"Awfully jolly—as cold as ice; come along."

And in a few minutes all six children were waddling about in the not very clear water, for the stirred-up mud at the edge had quite spoiled the look of things for the time being, and I am sure the waterfowl, and the fish, and even the water-rats were extraordinarily frightened at the strange things that were happening, poor dears!

All went well, or fairly well, for some time, though little Leigh's face began to look very blue, and his teeth chattered, and but for his fear of being thought a baby, I rather think he would have begun to cry.

Helena did not notice him for some time; she was feeling a little giddy and queer herself, and found it not too easy to keep her skirts, short as they were, out of the water, and herself on her feet. There were some sharp pebbles among those that made the bed of the stream, and she had never before tried walking barefoot out of doors, even on a smooth surface, and therefore found it very difficult.

But when at last she happened to catch sight of her little brother, she started violently and nearly lost her balance. "Go back at once, Leigh," she cried. "Look at him, Freda—he's all white and blue."

Freda was a kind-hearted girl, and she too was startled.

"I'll take him to the bank—he'll be all right when I've rubbed his feet," she exclaimed, and she hurried forward. But for all her good intentions she only made matters worse.

Instead of taking hold of the child to help him, she managed to push him over—and in another second Leigh was floundering in the mud at the edge of the little stream!

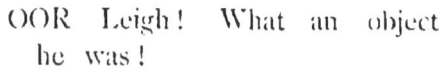

Part 3

POOR Leigh! What an object he was!

At first the three Kingleys burst out laughing.

But when Helena and Willie turned upon them sharply, they quickly grew serious, for they were far from unkind children, and the sight of their little friend's real distress and fear made them anxious to help to put things to right.

"He's as white as a sheet," said Helena, who was almost in tears. "And shivering so. Oh! Leigh dear, do you feel very bad?"

"N-no, don't cry, Nelly," said the little boy. "It's—it's my jacket and knickerbockers I mind about."

Freda turned him round promptly.

"It's only on one side," she said; "and a lot of it will brush off the jacket, at least, and after all, the knicker-bockers can be washed. What I mind about is you're shiver-ing so. Sit down, young man—here's a nice dry place, and I'll give your feet a good rub."

So she did, using for that purpose one of her brother
Hugh's long rough stockings, quite heedless of his grumbling.
She was certainly a very energetic girl. In a few minutes
Leigh's feet were in a glow, and the colour crept back to
his face again, and he left off shivering.

"There now," she said, "you are all right again, or at
least you will be, when you've run home and got a clean
jacket. After all, you're quite dry underneath—the mud is
thick and hasn't soaked through. Now, what had we best
do, Nelly?"

"Get him home as quick as possible some back way,
so that we won't meet anyone, I should say," said Hugh,
as he drew on his stockings, very glad to have recovered
his property.

But just as he spoke, there came a well-known sound
—well known at least to the Frere children, for it was their
Mother's voice calling them.

"Nell-ly! Nell-ly! Will-ie! Will! where are you?" it
said.

They looked at each other.

"It's Mamma," said Willie.

"What can have made her come out so soon?" said
Helena. "She was going to wait till the other ladies came
to tea, and then she said she and Sybil would stroll out
with them, and see what we were doing in the garden.
But I never thought they'd come down here—we scarcely
ever do, 'cos Nurse thinks we'll fall into the water."

Nurse's fears were not without reason, were they?

"We mustn't be seen like this," said Freda, "that's cer-
tain. Let's crouch in here quite quietly for a minute or
two, till they're out of the way—don't speak or anything.
Hush! perhaps we can hear their voices."

Hiding from Mamma was a new experience to Helena

and her brothers, and they did not like the feeling of it.
But just now there was nothing else to do, and Freda had
taken it all into her own hands. So they did as she said.

No sound of voices reached them for some moments,

but they heard footsteps overhead. Several people were
crossing the bridge. "Goodness gracious," said Freda, in a
whisper, "we've only just hidden ourselves in time. Do
come closer, and don't speak, whatever you do," though no
one had been speaking but herself.

Then the steps stopped, and a faint murmur was heard, but not loud enough to distinguish the words; and then the newcomers' steps moved on again.

The children began to breathe more freely.

"Better stay quiet another minute or two," said Freda.

But Helena was not happy in her mind about little Leigh.

"It's so damp and chilly in here under the bridge," she said to Freda. "He's sure to catch cold unless he gets a run in the sunshine."

"He must be awfully delicate then," said Hugh, with some contempt in his voice. "You should see the wettings *we* get—even Maggie, and she's a *girl*."

At this Leigh grew very red, and Helena found he was going to burst out crying, which would not have been a very good way of showing he was a man, I consider.

But Freda told Hugh not to talk nonsense, for she was sensible enough to know that what Helena said was true.

"I'll peep out now," she said, "and if the coast is clear, I'll 'cooey' to you very softly, like we do at 'I spy,' and then you can all come out. I'll wait for you at the top of the bank. It's a bother to go up it and down and up again—it's such slippery work."

She peeped out as she said—cautiously at first; then again encouraged, she made her way half way up the bank and glanced round her.

It seemed safe enough.

The group of ladies was to be seen at some little distance now; they were returning towards the house by the proper road, which it would be easy for the children to avoid.

And in her satisfaction, Freda gave a loud "cooey"— much louder than was needed, as her companions were close by.

Out popped all the heads from below the bridge, but before their owners had time to begin to climb the bank, they were stopped by a "Hush," and an energetic shake of the head from Freda, who next, greatly to their surprise, flopped straight down among the high grass at the top, and lay there motionless and quite flat.

The reason of this was soon explained. Again came the cry—"Nell-y! Will-ie! Nell-y!" from Mrs. Frere, and a whistle, which Hugh Kingley whispered to the others was his sister Sybil's.

"They've heard Freda's 'cooey,'" he said. "What a goose she was to call so loud!"

Again there was nothing for it but to stay quiet, which was becoming very tiresome.

The Frere children began to think that their ideas of "great fun," and the Kingleys', did not at all agree.

"Wasting all the afternoon in this nasty damp hole, and risking Leigh's getting really ill," thought Helena.

And at last she sprang up and called out to Freda.

"I won't stay here any longer," she cried. "Whether we are scolded or not, I won't. It isn't safe for Leigh."

"How cross you are!" said Freda coolly. "I was just going to tell you to come out. I think it's all right now; they've moved on. We can make a rush for the house across the grass somehow, can't we? There must be some back way in, where we shouldn't meet anyone. Then you and I can take Leigh up to the nursery and say he had an accident, which is quite true—and when he's clean again he can come out to us and your Mamma needn't know anything about it. The rest of us are all quite tidy—quite as tidy as can be expected after running about."

Helena did not reply. She was feeling too annoyed and vexed, and she did not like Freda's wish to hide what had really caused their troubles.

But she took Leigh by the hand—Freda, it must be allowed, taking him kindly by the other, and they all set off as fast as they could to the house. They could not go quite straight for fear of being seen; they had to "dodge" once or twice, but in the end they got safely there without meeting anyone more formidable than a tradesman's cart driving away from the stables, or an under-gardener laden with a basketful of vegetables.

Nurse looked grave, as she well might do, when she saw Leigh's plight. But Freda had a very pleasant bright manner, and Nurse was quite satisfied with her explanations.

And as the run home had brought back the colour to the little boy's cheeks, nothing much was said as to the fear of his having caught cold.

Part 4

OME half an hour or so afterwards, all the party, the children included, assembled on the lawn for tea.

Nurse had seized the opportunity of Helena's running in with Leigh, to "tidy her up a bit," and Freda too had not objected to a little setting to rights, so that both the girls looked quite in order.

And Willie and Hugh had also removed all traces of their adventures; only Maggie was still rather rumpled and crumpled, but as she was counted a tom-boy at all times, it did not so much matter.

"What became of you all, this afternoon?" asked Mrs. Frere. "We walked down to the bridge to look for you, as one of the men said he had seen you going that way. And I am *sure* I heard one of you 'cooeying'—did I not? Yet when I called, no one replied."

5

The children looked at each other. Mrs. Frere felt surprised.

"What is the mystery?" she said, though with a smile.

"Oh," began Freda, "there wasn't any mystery—we were only——" She stopped, for she felt that Helena's eyes were fixed on her, and Freda was not by nature an untruthful child. It was through her heedlessness and wildness that she often got into what she would have called "scrapes," from which there seemed often no escape but by telling falsehoods, or at least allowing what was not the case to be believed.

She grew red, and Mrs. Frere, feeling that it was not very kind to cross-question a guest, finished her sentence for her.

"Hiding?" she said. "Were you hiding?" though she wondered why Freda should blush and hesitate about so simple a thing.

"Yes," said Helena quickly, replying instead of Freda, "yes, Mamma, we *were* hiding—under the bridge."

At the moment she only felt glad to be able to say what *in words* was true.

For hiding they certainly had been. And Mrs. Frere, thoroughly trusting Helena, turned away and thought no more about it, only adding that it must have been rather dirty under the bridge; another time she would advise them to find a cleaner place.

"I suppose it was 'I spy' you were playing at," she said, and she did not notice that no one answered her.

The rest of the afternoon passed quietly enough.

Hugh and Freda were rather unusually quiet, at which their Mother and elder sister rejoiced.

"I do hope," said Sybil, as she drove home with Mrs. Kingley, leaving the younger ones to follow as they had come, "I do hope those Frere children, though they are younger, will have a good influence upon Hugh and the girls, Freda especially. She has been getting wilder and wilder. And Helena is such a lady-like, well-bred little girl."

"I hope so too," said her Mother. "I own I was a little afraid of our children startling the Freres, but they seem to have got on all right."

"Good night, dears," said Mrs. Frere to her three

children an hour or so later. "You were happy with your new friends, I hope? I think they seem nice children, and they were very quiet and well-behaved to-day. Leigh, my boy, you look half asleep—are you very tired?"

"My eyes are tired," said Leigh, "and my head, rather."

"Well, off with you to bed, then," she said cheerfully. She would not have felt or spoken so cheerfully if she could have seen into her little daughter's heart.

Nurse too noticed that Leigh looked pale and heavy-eyed.

She said she was afraid he had somehow caught cold. So she gave him something hot to drink after he was in bed, and soon he was fast asleep, breathing peacefully.

"He can't be very bad," thought Helena, "if he sleeps so quietly."

But though she tried not to be anxious about him, she herself could not succeed in going to sleep.

She tossed about, and dozed a little, and then woke up again—wider awake each time, it seemed to her. It was not *all* anxiety about Leigh; the truth was, her conscience was not at peace; she felt as if she deserved to be anxious about her little brother, for she saw clearly now, how she had been to blame—first, for giving in to the Kingleys in doing what she knew her Mother would not have approved of, and besides, and even worse than that—in concealing the wrong-doing, and telling what was "not quite true" to her trusting Mother.

The tears forced their way into Helena's eyes when she owned this to herself, and at last she felt that she could bear it no longer.

She got softly out of bed without waking Nurse, and made her way to the little room where Willie slept alone.

"Willie," she said at the door, almost in a whisper, but Willie heard her. He, too, for a wonder, was not able to sleep well to-night, and he at once sat straight up in bed.

"Yes, Nelly," he said, in a low, though frightened voice, "what is it? Is Leigh ill?"

"No," Helena replied; "at least, I hope not, though I'm awfully unhappy about him. It's partly that and partly—everything, Willie—all we did this afternoon. And

worst of all," and here poor Nelly had hard work to choke
down a lump that began to come in her throat, "I didn't
tell Mamma the truth, when she asked what we were
doing, you remember, Willie."

"Yes," said Willie, "I remember. You said we were
hiding, and so we were."

"But it wasn't quite true the way I let her think it,"
persisted Helena. "Even if the words were true, the *thinking*
wasn't. And it has made me so dreadfully unhappy. I didn't
know how to wait till the morning to tell her —I know I
shan't go to sleep all night," and she did indeed look very
white and miserable.

Willie considered; he had good ideas sometimes, though
Helena often called him slow and stupid.

"I know what," he said. "You shall write a letter to
Mamma—now, this minute. I've got paper and ink and pens
and everything, in my new birthday writing-case, and
I've got matches. Since my birthday, Papa said I might
have them in my room."

For Willie was a very careful little boy. If there was
no likelihood of his "setting the Thames on fire," his
Father had said once, "there was even less fear of his
setting the *house* on fire," and though Willie did not quite
understand about the "Thames"—how could a *river* burn?—
he saw that Papa meant something nice, so he felt quite
pleased.

And the next morning, the first thing Mrs. Frere saw
on her toilet-table was a note addressed rather shakily in
pencil, to "dear Mamma."

It was only a few lines, but it made her hurry to throw
on her dressing-gown and hasten to the nursery.

"How is Leigh?" were her first words to Nurse.

"He's got a little cold in his head, ma'am, but nothing

"Willie at once sat straight up in bed."

much," was the cheerful reply, and Mamma saw by the child's face that there were no signs of anything worse.

"But, Miss Helena," Nurse went on, "has had a bad night, and her head is aching, so I thought it better to keep her in bed to breakfast."

Poor Nelly! she had not much appetite for breakfast, and the first thing she did when Mamma's dear face appeared at the door was to burst into tears.

But such tears do good, and still more relief was the telling the whole story, ending up with—

"Oh, Mamma, dear Mamma, I couldn't bear to think I had told you what was *not quite true*. And Willie feels just the same."

For Willie had crept in too, looking very grave, and winking his eyes hard to keep from crying.

It was all put right, of course; there was really no need for their Mother to show them where they had been wrong. They knew it so well. And Leigh did not get ill, after all.

Freda Kingley had had a lesson too, I am glad to say.

That very afternoon she and Hugh walked over to Halling Park, to "find out" if Leigh was all right.

And this gave Mrs. Frere a good opportunity of showing the kind-hearted but thoughtless children the risk they had run of getting themselves and their little friends into real trouble—above all, by concealing their foolish play, and causing Nelly and her little brothers for the first time in their lives to act at all deceitfully.

"You will be afraid to let them play with us any more," said Freda very sadly, "and I'm sure I don't wonder."

"No, dear," said her new friend. "On the contrary, I shall now feel sure that I *may trust* you and Hugh and Maggie."

G148660

Freda grew red with pleasure.

"You may indeed," she said; "I promise you we won't lead them into mischief and—and if ever we do, we'll tell you all about it at once."

Mrs. Frere laughed at this quaint way of putting it.

"I don't think my children will be any the worse for a little more 'running wild' than they have had," she said.

"And we won't be any the worse for having to think a little before we rush off on some fun," said Freda. "I really never did see before how very easy it would be to get into telling regular *stories,* if you don't take care."

In The Chimney Corner

by

Frances E. Crompton

"IT'S a welly anxictious thing, roasting chestnuts is,"
Rupert said, shaking his head seriously.

Rupert is only four years old, but he is very
fond of grand words. He speaks quite plainly and
nicely, Nurse says (excepting the *v*'s and *r*'s), only, of course,
he cannot remember always just the shape of the big words;
but he uses much grander ones than I do, though I am
nearly six.

But he is the nicest little boy in all the world, and we
do love each other better than anybody else at all, after
Mother and Father.

We made what Rupert calls an "arranglement" about
always being friends with each other; that was the night
we roasted the chestnuts.

6

It was one of the most interesting things we had ever done—and then to be allowed to do it alone! You see, this was the way.

It was the dreadfullest day we can remember in all our lives.

Because you know, first of all, Mother was so ill. And then there was a birthday party we were to have gone to.

And Sarah, who is the housemaid, said she didn't see why we couldn't go just the same, and Nurse said very sharply :

"I'm not going to let them go, I can tell you, with things as they are."

And then she said, in another kind of voice:

"Just suppose they had to be sent for to go in to the mistress——"

And then she went away again into Mother's dressing-room.

That was another horrid thing, that nobody seemed to be able to look after us at all; we could have got into all sorts of mischief if we had wanted, but everything was so dreadful that it made us not want.

There were two doctors, who went and came several times, and someone they called Nurse, but she wasn't *our* Nurse.

And our Nurse could not be in the nursery with us, but kept shutting herself up in Mother's dressing-room, and that made us be getting into everybody's way.

So at last, when evening came, Nurse sent us down to the drawing-room, because somebody had let the nursery fire go almost out, and she told us to stay there and be good, and Father said he would perhaps come and sit with us by-and-by.

But I don't know what we should have done there so

long if Sarah had not brought us a plate of chestnuts, and shown us how to roast them.

(We feel sure that Nurse would not have allowed it by ourselves, and would have called it "playing with fire," but Father looked in at us once, and did not stop us at all, but only said we were very good, and Cook and Sarah kept

looking in too, and they were very kind, only rather quiet and queer.)

So that was how it was that we came to be allowed to be roasting chestnuts in the drawing-room by ourselves, which does seem a little funny, if you did not know about that dreadful day.

"There's only two left now," Rupert said.

We hadn't eaten all the plateful, of course, because so many of them, when they popped, had popped quite into the fire, and we were not to try to get them out.

We had roasted one each for Sarah, and for Cook, and for Nurse, and for Father, and of course the biggest of all for Mother.

We thought she might enjoy it when she got better. And they were all done, and there were only two left besides what we had eaten and lost.

So we put them together on the bar to roast, and Rupert said:

"One for you, and one for me. Yours is the light one, and mine is the dark one."

And I said:

"Yes, and let us do them as Sarah did with two of them, and try if they will keep together till they are properly done, and then it will be as if we kept good friends and loved each other always."

So that was what Rupert called the "anxietious" part, because, you know, one of them might have flown into the fire before the other was roasted, and we were so excited about it that I believe we should have cried.

But they were the nicest chestnuts of all the plateful, and that was the nicest thing of all that long day that had so many nasty ones in it.

For the dark chestnut and the light one kept together all the time, and split quite quietly and comfortably, and began to have a lovely smell, and then we thought it was fair to rake them off.

"Those chestnuts were welly fond of each other," said Rupert, in his solemnest way, while they were cooling in the fender. "Like you and me, Nella."

"And so we'll promise on our word-of-honours to be

"Rupert knelt down on the rug."

friends like them and love each other for always and always,"
I said.

And we held each other's hands, and when the chestnuts
were cooled and peeled, ate them up, and enjoyed them most
of all the chestnuts.

But after we had made that play last as long as we could,
and it grew later and later, it began to seem miserabler than
ever.

And nobody came to take us to bed, although it did
feel so dreadfully like bedtime, and nobody brought us any
bread-and-milk, and chestnuts do not really make a good supper,
even if you have roasted them yourself. And I tried to tell
Rupert "The Steadfast Tin Soldier," but he grew cross because
I couldn't tell it as well as Mother.

So I said:

"Well, let us lie down here on the rug, and perhaps if
we make believe, it will seem like going to bed."

But Rupert said, how could he go to bed without saying
his prayers, and he was so tired and cross that I said:

"Well, you say yours, and I'll hear them."

And so Rupert knelt down on the rug, and said his
prayers, and I heard them; at least, I mean, we tried; but
I couldn't always remember what came next, and then *he*
remembered that he wanted Mother, and burst out crying.

So I did not know what to do any more, and I could
only huggle him, as he calls it, and wipe his eyes on my
frock, and we sat there and huggled each other.

And I think we fell asleep in the chimney corner after
that.

At least, the next thing we remember is being picked up
by Father and Nurse, and Nurse carried Rupert upstairs, and
Father carried me.

And I said:

"We've tried to be good, Father, but we were obliged to go to sleep on the floor—just there; we really and truly couldn't keep awake any longer."

And Father did not think it naughty, I am sure, for he kissed us both ever so many times at the nursery door, with a great big hug, although he went away without speaking.

And Nurse undressed us as quickly as she could, and as Rupert calls it, "'scused" our baths, for we were so dreadfully sleepy; and I did think once that Nurse seemed to be crying, but I was too tired to notice any more.

And that was the end of the dreadfullest day we have ever known.

It began to be happier quite soon next day, for Granny came, and stayed with us, and had time to love us very much.

We told her about the chestnuts, and she thought it ever so nice.

And she told us something too, two things, and one was very beautiful, and one was very dreadful.

And the beautiful thing was that God had sent us a baby sister on that dreadful evening. But then He saw that He could take better care of her than even Mother and Nurse, and He loved her so much that He sent an angel to fetch her away again.

And though we were sorry not to have the little sister (and that was another reason to make Rupert and me love each other all the more, Granny said), yet she told us how beautiful it was to know that Baby Lucy would never do a naughty thing, or say a naughty word, but always be kept quite safe now.

And the dreadful thing was—but I can only say it in a

whisper—that God had almost taken *Mother* away, to be with Baby Lucy too.

But He looked down at us, and at Father, Granny said, and was sorry for us; and I think the time when He was sorry was when Rupert was crying, and I was trying to hear his prayers, because He must have seen that I could not be like Mother to Rupert, not however much I tried.

And so He was sorry for us, and Mother stayed.

www.ingramcontent.com/pod-product-compliance
Lightning Source LLC
Chambersburg PA
CBHW022202020726
47496CB00008B/2844

9 7 8 3 3 3 7 2 2 7 8 4 5